Tales from Duckport

Trick or Treat?
Neat!

by Suzy Spafford

SCHOLASTIC INC.
New York   Toronto   London   Auckland   Sydney
Mexico City   New Delhi   Hong Kong   Buenos Aires

Copyright © 2002 Suzy Spafford.
All rights reserved. Published by Scholastic Inc.

Suzy's Zoo, Suzy Ducken, Jack Quacker, Corky Turtle, Penelope O'Quinn, Emily Marmot,
Ollie Marmot, Vivian Snortwood, Cornelia O'Plume, Grandma Gussie, Duckport, and
associated logos and character designs are trademarks and service marks of Suzy's Zoo
in the United States and other foreign countries.

SCHOLASTIC and associated logos are
trademarks and/or registered trademarks of Scholastic Inc.

ISBN 0-439-38356-0

Cover design by Keirsten Geise.
Interior design by Robin Camera.

10 9 8 7 6 5 4 3 2 1   02 03 04 05

Printed in the U.S.A.
First Scholastic printing, August 2002

TABLE OF CONTENTS

Fall's a Ball!   5

One Big Happy Costume   17

We Love a Parade!   29

Many, many years ago, two brothers discovered the Beak Isles. Their names were Tim Duck One and Tim Duck Two. Tim Duck Two started the town of Duckport there. To this day, pictures of this fearless explorer can be seen all over town. How many can you find?

FALL'S A BALL!

"Marmot Farm is the best!"
exclaimed Suzy Ducken.
And she was right.
Marmot Farm was the best place of
all to enjoy fall!

"Like I always say," Grandma Gussie began, "a trip to Marmot Farm this morning means . . ." "Apple pie this afternoon!" the children cheered.

Suzy and the gang headed into
the orchard.
Everyone had a different way to
pick apples.

Suzy and Emily wanted to find
perfect apples.
An hour passed.
Suzy looked in their basket.
"Maybe we're being a little too
picky," she decided.

9

Jack and Corky
used teamwork.
Jack did the
shaking.
Corky did the
catching.
"It looks like you
got a head start on
making applesauce!"
Jack laughed.

Sally made herself the official apple taster.

"Mushy, with a hint of . . . worms!"
she shrieked.

Next it was time to choose
pumpkins.
The girls picked small cute ones.
The boys chose big round ones.

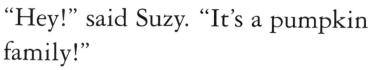

"Hey!" said Suzy. "It's a pumpkin family!"

"And look!" Emily added. "Twins!"

"I've got the granddaddy of them all!" declared Ollie.

Grandma Gussie borrowed a wagon.
Back home, there was a lot to
unload—including six pooped
pickers!

Later, the kids began to carve the
pumpkins.
"I can't wait to see them!"
said Grandma Gussie.
"You kids are always so creative!"

"Ready!" the kids announced proudly.
They revealed their jack-o'-lantern faces.
"This **must** be a pumpkin family!"
Grandma Gussie declared.
"They look so much alike!"

ONE BIG HAPPY COSTUME

"Let's go to the attic!" announced
Grandma Gussie.
Suzy and her friends cheered.
There was so much cool stuff up
there!

Suzy and Sally's mom came to
join in the fun.
Lizzie Ducken loved Halloween.
She pretended to be a witch.

She let out a terrible shriek.
Suzy laughed.
"That's the same sound you make
when my room is a mess!"

Suzy put on the first costume
pieces she found.
"How do I look?" she asked.
"Confused!" Jack answered.

Emily discovered a feather headdress.

"I'm a princess fairy!" she said
dreamily.
"Or a fairy princess. Whichever is
fancier."

"Roar!" shouted Ollie.
"Awwww! How cute!" said Suzy
and Sally.

"I am not cute!" Ollie said.
He looked as if he might cry.
"I am a terrifying lion!"

Jack tried on stilts.
It was a good thing that Grandma
Gussie had an old mattress in her attic.

23

Sally put on a pink tutu.
"Hey!" she said. "I'm a trapeze
artist!"

"Of course!"
said Grandma
Gussie.
"You can all be
a circus troupe!"

"I'll be the ringmaster!"
shouted Suzy.
Ollie growled.
He wanted to be a
terrifying lion.

"I'll be a lion tamer!" Emily
declared.

"I can be a juggler," offered Corky,
"with some practice."
"And I'll be the tallest guy
on earth!" exclaimed Jack.
"Whooaah!"

"This is going to be
great!" said Suzy.
"We'll need a tent.
And circus music. And—"

27

"All you'll need," said her mother,
"is to smile and say 'trick or treat!'"

WE LOVE A PARADE!

It was Halloween at last!
Suzy and her pals were so excited.

Soon they were ready to go
trick-or-treating.

"Now remember to smile," Emily
ordered.
"A circus is meant to bring joy to
children young and old."
"Oh, brother!" moaned Jack.

First they headed straight for the bakery. Mrs. Angelfood gave them pumpkin cookies and juice.

"Aren't you cute?" she said to Ollie. "Grrrrrrr!" Ollie replied.

At the florist's shop, Miss Mulch said, "I hope that adorable lion doesn't gobble anyone up!"
Ollie looked as if he might bite her head off for real!

Outside, the kids bumped into
Penelope.
"What are you supposed to be?"
Suzy wondered.
"Monster Foot?" tried Penelope.

"I waited until the last minute.
This was all the store had left,"
she said sadly.
"I think we can help," said Suzy.
"Come here, everybody."

"There!" Suzy announced.
"Our circus was missing the most
important thing of all—a clown!"

The big costume parade was about
to begin.

Grandma Gussie and Mrs. Ducken
handed the kids a large banner.
"Surprise!" they both yelled.

The circus was the hit of the parade.

The judges even came up with a
new prize.
It was called "Best Bunch of
Costumes That All Go Together."

"With a treat like this," said Suzy,
"who needs candy?!"